# Ten Seconds To Midnight

## Connor Burrough

Copyright © 2021 Connor Burrough All rights reserved

The characters and events portrayed in this book are fictitious. Any similarity to real persons, living or dead, is coincidental and not intended by the author.

No part of this book may be reproduced, or stored in a retrieval system, or transmitted in any form or by any means, electronic, mechanical, photocopying, recording, or otherwise, without express written permission of the publisher.

ISBN: 9798669248901

Written with Special thanks to Adrienaholic, SilhouetteNimiane, StimpackPrincess and PartyOfNinjas for their help in keeping me sane this past while

## Chapter 1

It was two in the morning as he lay there, listening to the sounds of the night; a light September rain outside whispering into the trees, and playing amongst the blades of grass outside - the rushing of the wind and the subsequent slight bend in the windows as it reached its crescendo, whining into the fading paint of the old wooden window frames. He focused on the small noises, such as the quiet, rhythmic movements in the cloth bedding upon which he lay, synchronising with the slightly strained breathing of his wife, who lay sleeping next to him. The noises faded away into the darkness, only to be swiftly replaced with a high-pitched droning. He clapped his hand gently against the side of his head, quickly silencing the ringing that emanated from inside his head. Everything was still, sombre, soundless - and yet somehow, the boundless void of silence and darkness outside was soothing in a way.

The sun had just crawled its way over the horizon as the old man rose, having been awoken by his wife. He lifted himself gently up onto his legs, seemingly as decrepit as the house in which he resided. However, he'd never bring himself to admit it, instead opting for the classic, British 'Stiff upper lip' approach he grew up with. He dressed and wandered downstairs, taking his time about it; after all, he did have all day. He followed the hard wooden floor out into the kitchen, closing the door to the guest room that stood slightly ajar as he passed. The kitchen was rural and straightforward; the only modern appliances filling it were a gas stove and a fridge. A fireplace stood audaciously in the corner, quietly burning oak logs, warming the ceramic tiles that coated the floor in glossy shades of black and white; which were interrupted only by the dining table; which stood like a stoic island in the middle of the sea.

The kitchen filled with a plethora of smells as his wife cooked breakfast – thickly cut bacon with eggs, a time honoured Saturday morning tradition. He sat at the table and turned on the radio as he picked up the morning's paper. "Morning" he started, being swiftly interrupted as the radio burst into life with the usual dregs: talk shows, music channels, the weather – the latter being a particular favourite target for his lambasting, with most people agreeing with his sentiment; why do they need someone to tell them the weather when they can look out the window?

"The news won't be on for another quarter-hour", Eva reminded him as she placed two plates on the table and seated herself, being careful not to trap her dress beneath herself – creases would never do; one must always be presentable for guests. He began to reach for the radio, to switch it off to enjoy his breakfast without this rabble when it put out something useful. "It has now been confirmed that the 'Red Menace' of Russia has a nuclear arsenal. Citizens are advised to make sure they have ready access to a shelter. Government-approved pamphlets have been distributed and can be collected from centres erected in towns, cities, and villages across the country".

His hand hung in mid-air, hovering just in front of the switch for the radio, intent on taking in as much information as possible; however, he was quick to switch it off when the broadcast returned to its usual music and other rubbish.

His wife pointed her knife at the radio - "If you're headed into town to pick up one of those, can you grab a loaf of bread from James for me? He should have opened by the time you get there".

He nodded, knowing his wife (or "the ol' ball and chain" as he preferred to say; although only when she wasn't in earshot, else she'd have a stick across his legs for saying it), wouldn't be best pleased if he didn't obey. He finished his breakfast and stood slowly, carrying their plates to the sink, before starting across the room to grab his coat – a vast trek across the room and like a noble explorer, he journeyed on valiantly.

He grabbed a light jacket – brown fabric with long sleeves. It hung loosely on him and a tad lower than a jacket should fall on his small, crooked frame, but he didn't mind. It served him well and had done so for years. He sauntered down toward the front door – closely followed by his wife, as he mentally prepared himself to deal with that hooligan James, the baker in town. What reason does anyone have to smile continually? Stephen was happy, but he didn't have to have everyone know it.

Eva straightened his jacket, zipping it up for him before kissing him goodbye; "What would I do without you, Darling".

She smiled at him and pinned a grocery list to his lapel - "Be safe, Stephen, I hear the teenagers are about in the town again, harassing people with those fliers for the church bake sale".

He gave her an understanding nod before unlatching the door and heading out, down the rarely used driveway toward the bus stop.

The house was rather large for the period in which it was built, with a grand total of two floors, yet there weren't too many rooms that would leave them unable to keep up with the cleaning. It stood as a lone bulwark against the world, a sole light in a sea of darkness, defiantly sitting upon a slight incline in the middle of nowhere, about ten minutes from the nearest town. The winding driveway led down onto the road, though it was seldom used – they didn't need a car; they preferred to walk anyway, and if it was too far to walk, the bus would go there. If there wasn't a bus that went there, it obviously wasn't a place worth visiting.

The bus stop lay just beyond the reaches of the long gravel driveway. It was a modest affair, consisting entirely of one impressive lone rusty pole with a small sign showing the bus times. Stephen spent a significant amount of time standing near to or gently meandering around in the general vicinity of that pole, often sopping wet while doing so. Oymor Bay council never cared to put a shelter nearby, despite this being England - where it rains far too often, except for in the few days of summer which come around sometimes. As Eva often remarked, he spent more time around that pole than around Mark, though he was often quick to dismiss these allegations with a hand wave - he did have to work after all. He dismissed these thoughts as he checked his pockets - wallet, check. Loose change? Check; he made a mental note to get rid of a bit of the shrapnel he was carrying; it was inconvenient moving so many coins. He boarded the metal box which stood before him. The bus seemed almost as dilapidated as his house was, with windows that rattled under the force of the engine and tires that could do with some love. Stephen exchanged the usual pleasantries with the driver before collapsing into his regular seat - right at the front, aisle seat - to ensure he'd be left alone on the deserted bus.

## Chapter 2

The bus shuddered slowly into action, trundling along the quiet roads, dragging itself along like a dying animal as birds decided to make a quick escape from the hedges nearby. It was good enough for Stephen; he didn't need anything fancy to get him from point A to B. The seats were uncomfortable, and the thick soupy atmosphere inside made it feel as if one was stepping onto another planet - one that smells a tad like urine, unfortunately, but he could tolerate that. He had, after all, spent most of the latter part of his life riding the bus into town. It might smell like piss, but it was a second home to him.

The dilapidated relic of a bus made short work of what seemed to be an epic quest along the winding road into town. The hedges lining the streets blurred into a green mess of aromatic leaves and flowers, with the odd few hedgehogs and foxes scattered throughout as the bus lurched and shuddered along its path. However, the hedges and gnarled oak trees that stretch their arms toward the sky quickly gave way to cottages and small businesses as the bus reached the small seaside town. Another metal pole, which was in somewhat better condition than the one at home, appeared in front of them as the bus screeched its complaints before slowing to a halt with a chilling hiss, almost as if it were spitting in disdain at the passengers about to disembark. "Oymor Bay".
His voice was gruff but betrayed a sense of tiredness, the type of long-dead boredom that comes from years of repetition in a job you stopped enjoying a long time ago.

It was a small town residing by the village, built to house the workers from the not particularly world-famous Rurdeau coal mine nearby. Some of the old wooden cottages still stood, although much of the town was abandoned and demolished, to make space for the expansion of farmland after the closing of the mine. Some residents, like Stephen, were particularly begrudged, however with no reason to stay around since the pit's closure, most were happy to leave their homes in search of a less dull place to live. Large gnarled oak trees dotted the streets, giving solace to the many birds and other creatures that lived in and around the small hamlet, occasionally to the annoyance of the townspeople, who were often woken to the sound of wood pigeons. Many of the people residing there were older, like Stephen, remnants of the old mining town, reluctant to leave due to the fear of change; however, no one would ever admit that. The few shops that remained were enough to satisfy the needs of those who stayed behind, whether it be the Boulangerie Bakery or the old Swan and Fox - which was a popular place for residents to go to profess their love for one another after getting particularly jolly; even the most reclusive residents could never resist the allure of a cold, crisp lager.

He slowly climbed down from the rusted old bus, taking the plunge onto the slightly warm concrete of the paving slabs that covered the majority of Oymor Bay. He greeted the smiling faces that passed with a nod, a common occurrence within the town, used when one has somewhere to go and doesn't want to end up stuck in a twenty-minute conversation about someone's grandchildren. He was on a mission: to acquire groceries and avoid the small population of teenagers in the town; those bastards are a menace, especially the ones who hang around the church. The bustled with activity, although it was typically a very slow bustle; the sound of feet shuffling across the pavement as people meandered around, smiling at Stephen as he passed, echoed throughout the streets, interrupted only by the occasional car passing through. Presumably, they were lost. Most people never have a reason to visit the town, although some will pass through on the way to other villages or the impeccably clean bay.

Stephen wandered into the Boulangerie Bakery, famous around town for its bread and cakes. However, he and Eva often wondered if that was *really* a bragging point, considering that bread and cakes are what bakeries specialise in. James, the town baker, greeted him with his familiar jovial tune: "Mornin' Walters! The usual fer you and the missus today?".
Stephen nodded in a dignified manner; "Just the one loaf today, for the old ball and chain",
A sly smile creeping across his face. James wrapped and weighed the loaf, laughing blithely; "don't let Eva hear you say that; she'll 'ave your legs! Be 30 pence anyway".
Stephen gave James a confused look. "Put your prices up?" He questioned as he handed the money over. James nodded with a murmur of agreement; "an extra sixpence for a laugh. Ted's charging bloody murder for flour this year though, must've been a bad harvest". Stephen gave an understanding look before taking his bread - poppy-seed bloomer, naturally, there was no better bread in his opinion - I best make a move then", he mumbled, "Need to grab one of them pamphlets".

James extended the usual formalities as Stephen wandered back out the door into the blinding sun - a far cry from the rain earlier in the morning.

A small stand with an equally diminutive man in a suit stood just outside the bakery, out on the warm cobblestones of the quiet street; the only indication of its purpose was the sign above reading "be prepared". Stephen took a pamphlet from the stand and carried on his way, skipping the usual pleasantries; the small man was, after all, an outsider, and as such, it was unclear if he could be trusted.

Cigarette butts and weeds line the side of the ill-used road, with the occasional group of pigeons gathering along the path before scattering upon Stephen's approach. A pair of youths in their Sunday best stood outside the small church; it was dedicated to Saint Lamberth – One Stephen had never heard of, though who was he to question it? The church was relatively small, compared to those in other towns, though it served its purpose. Reverend Parris had other ideas, seemingly dreaming of Cathedrals and golden candelabras instead of a small stone church in the middle of nowhere, without so much as a single stained window. The pair approached Stephen, offering him a modest flier, which he took instinctively; "looking to enter the competition this year, Mr Walters?" After a short pause, Stephen realised they were referring to the biannual church bake sale, which Parris made somewhat competitive, with the best selling cake garnering the baker a small trophy - one Eva seemed to win near effortlessly every time. "I'm sure the missus would love to - I didn't realise it was coming up on that time already".

He wandered away slowly, bidding farewell to the youths as he went, determined to reach the bus stop in proper time to be able to return home.

## Chapter 3

The bus slowly shuddered into the stop, barely missing the rusting, hole-ridden metal pole erected to evince the bus stop's existence. Stephen eventually managed to make his way from the bus's cold metal interior down onto the mildly warm black pavement that lay just shy of his driveway, clutching a small, brown paper bag of groceries. He started on an expedition up the slightly wet gravel of the driveway, the smell of petrichor rising as he disturbed the settled stones; the song of the birds chiming from the hedges that enclosed the house. The scene was suddenly shattered by the sound of the bus doors slamming closed behind him with a metallic clang, shortly before the bus hissed and spat before dragging itself down the road like a dying thing, carrying its miserable-looking passengers on toward wherever particularly catches their fancy.

With the passing of that infernal machine, peace returned to the area as the birds resumed their songs and the hedges continued to rustle in tune to the joyful whistle of the wind. The sound of Eva calling out quickly snapped Stephen out of his daze. He had, up until that point, been operating on a kind of autopilot, enjoying the nature around him; He hadn't even noticed the car parked in his driveway. Until he heard Eva calling out to the boy, that is. "How was the drive, Mark?".
How could he forget? The boy was coming over for the weekend to help them out as if he needed help. As far as Stephen was concerned, men should never ask for help - it isn't proper. Not that Mark would be of much use anyway,

with those posh middle-class hands of his, completely worthless compared to the hard, calloused, working man's hands Stephen found himself in possession of.

Mark had moved away from the quiet seaside town of Oymor Bay, searching for a 'better life' elsewhere, as if London would be a more pleasant place to live. From a young age, he'd made up his mind that he'd leave in search of better opportunities; the closure of the mine had been his signal to move on - Mark had seen how it left his father constantly tired and aching and decided that that wouldn't be how he'd live. Instead of staying in the small hamlet, he opted for a busier life in the city, working as an architect. This war came about just in time for Mark, offering the perfect excuse to visit his parents back in Oymor Bay - that Korean airliner being shot down a few weeks ago served as a convenient catalyst to this, giving him an excuse to see his mum.

He returned his mother's beckons with a smile and reassurance that he was feeling fine, extending a hug to the rapidly ageing woman - he may be almost thirty, but he would never be too old to hug his mother. However, his mood rapidly declined as he saw his father meandering up the driveway, seemingly in a daze. His eyes narrowed, and the warmth in his voice quickly drained away as he greeted the old man. "Father".

He tried his best to hide the sharpness to his tongue, at least while mum was around - in private, he could use the tense silences and sharp stares to express his disdain for the man.

Eva was quick to invite Mark inside, along with the alluring promise of a hot cup of tea, visibly eager to hear about what he'd been up to during his time away. Stephen and Mark seated themselves at the kitchen's dining table, occasionally exchanging dark glances, while Eva made the tea. She shortly found her seat and started grilling Mark about what he'd been up to and how the wife was. Stephen sat across the table, silently reading the booklet he picked up in town, save for the odd grunt of agreement. However, this was short-lived as Stephen quickly put down the pamphlet and decided to interrupt, ignoring Mark and focusing on Eva instead - "they're saying we should build a shelter, love. Out of doors and cushions".

Eva wrinkled her nose in response, "you best not go digging up my petunias out there, Stephen. I put a lot of work into those."

"No, up against the wall they're saying - I'll put them up in the living room. Shouldn't damage the wallpaper none".

Stephen struggled to his feet and set off for the backdoor; he never let anything go; it could come in handy one day, as much as Eva complained about the mess in the shed - this time, he was proven right at least. Mark placed his mug on the table, rising to his feet. "I'll lend a hand, couldn't leave you to do it on your own".

Stephen dismissed him with a hand wave, as he often had to while Mark was living at home - "With those piss-weak middle-class hands? You couldn't lift a cat flap, let alone a door".

He carried on his way out to the shed, leaving Mark to slowly sink back into his seat in frustration, not that he'd let it show in front of mum.

The doors were heavy and slightly splintered with age; it wouldn't be a pretty shelter, but Stephen was sure it would hold- the government had to know what they were doing after all, right? He struggled with each one, half carrying, half dragging them one by one through the house, leaning them against the wall. Although it wasn't part of the diagram, he decided to nail down a board to hold the doors in place; it'd probably be fine; surely, it could only help and not hinder. Mark and Eva chatted in the other room while Stephen traipsed around searching for cushions; the ones on the sofa would probably do. "Don't use my good cushions out of there!" Eva called out, making him jump slightly - "Bloody hell", he thought, "it's like she's bloody psychic".

He wandered upstairs and grabbed a few handfuls of cushions from the cupboard in the spare room. They'd have to do. A few on the outside like they suggested and a few for inside - if they were going to be hiding in a small space for a while, it may as well be a comfortable claustrophobic space.

"Right! That's that sorted then," he thought to himself, "Absolutely gasping for a drink".

Stephen made his way back into the kitchen, feeling proud of himself, before sitting back at the table with the paper to finish his tea - a fitting reward for a job well done. Although he would prefer it if that poxy radio weren't playing with the usual 'popular' music - whatever happened to the good old sports station? Almost as if someone out there had heard Stephen's thoughts of criticism, the music suddenly cut out, only to be replaced by a man's voice - "This is an emergency message to all citizens of this great nation of Britannia. Peace talks between the United States and Russia have broken down, leaving us all on the verge of war. Citizens are urged to be prepared, building shelters if

possible, as a pre-emptive strike in some capacity is expected from the USSR."
The message began to repeat itself, and so Stephen turned off the radio, leaving them all in silence for a moment as they reflected on what they just heard.

Eva was the first to break the silence - "Do you think writing a letter would help?".
Both Stephen and Mark looked over at her in confusion. "What if we wrote a letter to the Russian leader, asking them not to drop any bombs on us? I know I'm tired of being bombed after the last war".
Mark stifled a laugh and nodded silently; "Well, I'm sure it'd count for something, right? I mean-"
Stephen quickly cut him off - "The problem with that is, love. Is that them Jerries. I mean, them *Ruskies* are big, scary men. I don't think they'd exactly listen to reason considering their reputation for being ruthless is on the line".
Mark sighed silently, tired of being interrupted all the time while Eva mulled over the thought. "I might just write it anyway. See if it does anything".

Meanwhile, in an undisclosed location, a particularly scared-looking Russian soldier is fighting to maintain composure while rushing through endless corridors, pushing people out the way as he goes. There's one person he needs to talk to right now, and nothing else matters for the time being. Bursting through a set of large, heavy swing doors with all the grace of an incredibly clumsy brick, he called out into the large room before him (Translated into English for your convenience) "Lieutenant Colonel Petrov! I need to speak with Lieutenant Colonel Petrov!".

A large, surly man in uniform rose from a chair, turning to face the man; his chest decorated with medals and patches suggestive of his position of power - "What." he bellowed back, obviously irritated by the interruption. The soldier saluted his superior before addressing his question - "We've detected the launch of six American missiles. We need your express permission to retaliate with full force". Petrov fingered the cold metal key in his pocket - one of three required. His thoughts raced as he considered his options; an erroneous retaliatory strike would be suicide, wiping out near enough all life on the planet. However - he could not stand by and watch his country be destroyed before him by those damned Yanks. Swallowing hard and hoping the soldier who stood before him wasn't wrong, he made his way to locate two of his key-holding superiors.

## Chapter Four

The tense silence across the table, between Stephen and Mark, could be cut with a knife; or any other utensil for that matter - it was an unusually thick and gooey tense silence. The silence was broken only by faint distant sounds of a typewriter clacking away elsewhere in the house as Eva wrote her letter and the quiet music that remained playing in the background. Not even the birds outside dared to sing, lest their merry tune was to disturb the silence between the two men - such a transgression would be punishable by a politely quiet glare from Stephen. The chair upon which he sat didn't seem to understand this concept as it creaked loudly in response to every shift in weight as Stephen leaned in to change the station.

His hand stopped dead in the air in disbelief before he managed to accomplish this - an attention-grabbing alarm sounded from the small radio, interrupting the music broadcast before fading out to a particularly distressed-sounding man's voice. "There have been confirmed reports of nuclear launches from the USSR. My God."

He cleared his throat before continuing, obviously off-script, "I urge you all to take shelter wherever it is available, and stay away from windows. May God have mercy on us all".

The once tense silence dissolved into confusion, followed by a shared panic - encapsulated by the only words Stephen and Mark had said to each other in what felt like hours - "Fuck me. They've actually done it".

Mark was stood bolt-upright in a fraction of a second, sprinting out the room to collect his mother within another. Stephen managed to struggle to his feet and set about gathering any and all canned food he could - moving faster than he had in a long time as the all too familiar sirens wailed and screeched outside - the once silent streets of Oymor Bay erupted into screams of panic and wails, loud enough to reach them from the town. He dashed out of the kitchen, through the hallway and into the living room, being cut off by Mark before practically throwing the cans he was holding at Eva, who was hiding inside already - Mark moved his legs as fast as humanly possible, grabbing a metal bucket from under the stairs along with everything inside - it was unusually heavy. Still, Mark didn't have time to question that as he found his body suddenly lurching toward the shelter in what vaguely resembled a dive but could easily be mistaken for a baby bird trying to work out how to exist.

They sat in excruciating silence as the seconds passed, counting down to the inevitable - a loud banging emanated from the front door, along with screams and pleading and cries for help - Stephen was quick to shut down any notion anyone may have had about opening the door. "It's every man and woman for themselves now. We're in the midst of a war that's about to end - the best chance we have is in looking after our own. Even you, boy."

He regarded Mark with an incredibly frosty look. Mark didn't care; he was too busy to notice - being preoccupied with clutching the bucket to his chest and rocking back and forth rapidly. His thoughts raced, though each one passed too quickly for him to be able to pin any one down, except for one. Stephen seemed remarkably calm. He opened his mouth to say something, anything - "Fa-".

A blinding flash from outside quickly shut him up. They braced as the deafening crack rocked the house. The windows shattered, and the doors between them and an explosion of epic proportions rattled like leaves in a strong wind.

Outside, the damage was immeasurable. The shockwave rocked through the town. The church, which had stood for centuries, was ripped asunder in seconds - along with those who took refuge inside - the masses of stone and holy protection were nothing to the invisible force which burned them to ash in not so much as a fraction of a second. Hellfire ripped across the land, as everyone they had ever known or loved was brutally and senselessly destroyed; Eva could think only one thing "I think I left the oven on".

In completing the simple act of pushing a button, the USSR had not only just fired a volley of missiles but had seemingly opened an unholy portal to the darkest depths of hell - unleashing its inmates upon the unsuspecting world. As unimaginable heat shredded its way through the quiet fields, Mark's thoughts lay with his wife and child - his last words to her before leaving were downplaying the threat, reassuring her it'd all be okay. There'd have been no way they'd have survived - especially back in London. As the multiple automated retaliatory strikes landed on USSR soils and the lands of their allies, ripping through swathes of civilians - Stephen prayed. He prayed desperately to every divine entity he was aware of that even if he should perish, that Eva and the boy would survive. He'd never been a religious man - but in a situation as dire as this, it'd take a miracle. Or several. Though an unignorable voice in the back of his mind questioned what benevolent, all-powerful God would let this happen?


It was all over in seconds - though those seconds passed like years. A horrific, stomach-wrenching, purely vile smell perforated the air as the dust settled. A combination of burning wood and hair, charred grass and dirt; and one scent quite beyond comprehension - it turned Mark's stomach upside down, wrenching at his inside as he came to the slow realisation of what it was - a charred, overcooked meat smell - he listened for a second. The banging at the front door had stopped. No words could describe the abject horror that washed over Mark as he noticed - not only had the banging at the door stopped. All sound had, save for his retching and heavy breathing, had stopped. The wind that once blew through across the fields, dancing through the grass, stood still in solemn silence. The birds that once played and sung in the bushes, hedges and trees outside had stopped singing; there wasn't so much as a chirp to be heard. The bus that once crawled through the country lanes had fallen silent, having breathed its last shaky, toxic breath. Even Oymor Bay had fallen to the piercing silence that surrounded everything and seemingly bored into his very soul.

Mark ached all over and was flush with incredible fatigue, though it was him who first broke the seemingly impenetrable silence - though not with words of any kind. He lurched and staggered out of the makeshift shelter, quickly dropping to his knees and emptying the contents of his stomach, adding that familiar acidic, unmistakable smell to those already swirling around the room. With what energy he had left, Mark brought himself finally to look up at the house he grew up in - that he had so many memories in. The outside of the doors they were cowering behind were burnt to a crisp - the paint peeling as the wood beneath fell away in clumps. The sofa where he spent many a Saturday morning watching cartoons was burnt beyond any recognition - it had been showered in misshapen, half-melted shards of glass, much like most of the floor. The burnt remnants of his mother's homemade curtains lay strewn about the room, still smoking lightly - half smothered by the choking dust and ash that permeated the air like a foul perversion of the beautiful snowfall he played in as a child. He quickly motioned to his parents to stay inside before dragging himself across the singed remains of the wooden floor, collapsing in the entrance of their shelter, their saving grace - passing out to the sound of Eva's distraught screams and Stephen's shocked silence.

It took a moment for Stephen to process what had happened to his home properly. The once tranquil street was now a melted river of bubbling pitch and asphalt. The living room lay bare before him - that room where he once taught Mark to walk, where he heard his son's first words, where he proposed to Eva all those years ago. Where he promised that he'd protect her no matter what, while he had aimed to prove that chivalry wasn't as dead as God now seemed to be, how could he have possibly accounted for the extinction of the rest of the human race when he made that promise? Pictures had been knocked from the wall and shattered - precious, irreplaceable memories now turned into choking ash that fluttered effortlessly on the back of the hot, muggy air that pervaded everywhere and perverted everything it touched. On a rare few occasions, Stephen found himself at a complete and utter loss for words - this was one. He found himself filling with a deep, dark indescribable rage; it swirled inside him as he fought to choke it down - At that moment, Stephen wanted nothing more than to have the man who pressed that red button before him, to enact swift and efficient justice in ways that cannot be described within proper company. Never had he felt such a powerful, murderous urge. It scared the wits out of him, leaving him agape like a fish ripped from its natural habitat.

## Chapter Five

Mark came to laying on the floor where he fell - the sky outside burned with a dazzling red as if the Russians had set fire to the horizon. Hours had passed since Mark collapsed; he looked up to see Eva and Stephen sitting on what remained of the sofa, talking, as if their whole world hadn't been turned upside down mere hours ago. Mark gathered his strength and struggled to his feet, rubbing the bruise on his jaw as he shuffled over to join them. He immediately wished he hadn't. One look out the window showed the pure and unrivalled destruction of life - those lush fields that he once played in as a child now resembled a desert more than farmland, dotted with bovine 'cacti'. Mark dropped to his knees in despair; everyone was dead. "This is it".
He spoke softly, leaving the words to just drip from his mouth; "it's all gone. We're in the end times".
Eva looked over, her eyes betraying the hopelessness she was trying to hide. Stephen, however, was intently focused on the horizon - "Don't let the boy see you cry" was all he could think - "Men don't cry, Stephen".
Mark turned his gaze to the heavens - they were clearly visible through what remained of the upper floors of the house; "What now? What's next?" his voice cracked as tears rolled down his cheek silently.

Stephen, never one to admit he didn't know, resorted to his one and only hope - the pamphlet. "Well." He steeled his voice, not wanting to appear weak; "It says here... *At regular intervals, stimulate group activity*".

Eva furrowed her brow and managed to glare at him through the tears; "Don't you start stimulating, Stephen. I'm not in the mood".

Stephen suppressed a sigh; "I think they mean group games, poppet. To keep the house from going to Bedlam".

He paused, looking down at the crumpled paper in his hands. "We should keep track of what we have, so we can ration it, like in the war, love".

They collectively mumbled agreement - it was all there was to do; after all, there weren't many channels broadcasting through the apocalypse. They wandered aimlessly through the wreckage of the place they once called home, collecting what they could and depositing it in the living room. Stephen looked around at the pitiful bounty they had accumulated and rubbed his eyes; "Our supplies consist of; Three bottles of water, an expired tin of beans without an opener, and some strawberry jam".

He swallowed hard; these would barely last one person a few days, let alone three people for the rest of their lives. After some thought, he quickly settled on the fantastic plan of changing the subject - "Christ, my head is throbbing".

Eva concurred, "I do feel a mite dizzy myself".

He shook his head slightly - it must just be from being cooped up so long in the house; it was mighty warm out after all. "I'm going out for some fresh air", he offered, making his way to his feet. As if there wasn't enough fresh air coming in through that gaping hole in the wall that was once a window. Stephen wandered through the ashen remains of the kitchen toward the back door; "Don't be out there too long", Eva called out, "It's looking like rain; you'll catch your death out there!".

It was only once alone, in the garden, that Stephen finally comprehended the extent of the blast. "It'll be a bastard painting this house." he thought, "Once this is all over, that is".

The existential dread that plagued and hounded Mark's every thought was finally catching up to Stephen. What if they really were the last ones alive? Was this really the end for the human race? Should they give up and die? He pushed these thoughts to the far back of his mind. He had to be tough for the others to have any hope of keeping it together; the boy was useless, too foppish and posh in his opinion - and absolutely feckless. "I'll have to be harder on Mark." He mumbled to no one in particular, "It'll motivate him to be better!"

Stephen's aimless ponderings were quickly interrupted by Mark, as per usual. He was lugging a mass of pots and pans outside, dropping the majority of them onto the patio with a spectacular amount of noise - not that it mattered anymore anyway, there was no one around to hear them.

Mark looked up at his father blankly, he knew that Stephen would be fast to rain on his parade, yet he still tried nonetheless; "I'm going to collect the rainwater. We can go weeks without food, but water will be important".

The boy's fast thinking impressed Stephen, though he'd never let that on - if you told people every time they had a good idea, they'd get lazy and stop having them. He gave him the kind of distant nod one might give a stranger on the train and wandered inside, trying to find somewhere quiet so that he may think for a second. Mark carried on outside, spreading out the utensils across the patio and grass - occasionally scanning the horizon for any sign of life, no matter how slim the chances were. Something was moving out there, in those distant fields. It was tremendous and far from human. For a second, Mark swore that he and it locked eyes, despite the massive distance, and it did not look anywhere near friendly.

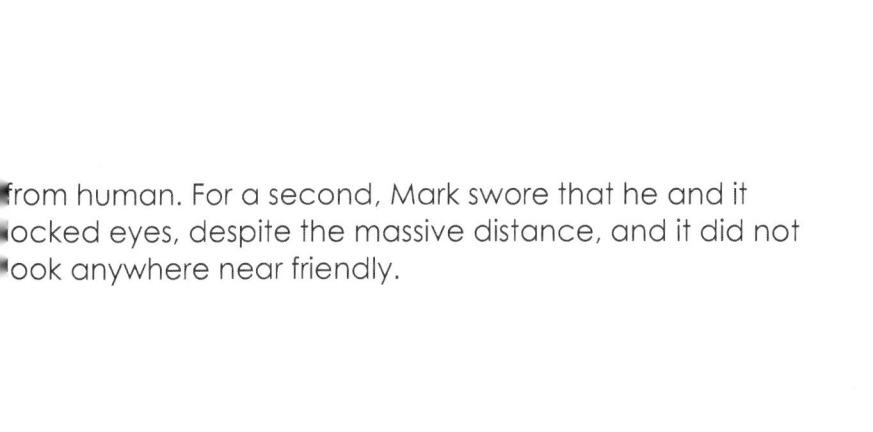

## Chapter Six

Stephen meandered back inside as black clouds rumbled in the distance; Eva was pottering about in the kitchen, clearly looking for something, but Stephen wasn't particularly interested in helping. He felt better than before and determined that having a sit-down was the best course of action, as any English gentleman should before thinking about whatever may trouble them. He practically collapsed into the lightly charred sofa, kicking up plumes of dust and launching small fragments of ceiling and charred pieces of glass off onto the floor. His gaze wandered about the room, assessing the damage before falling upon the entrance to the shelter.

He raised from the sofa slowly and wandered over to retrieve the radio from the shelter. The radio hadn't been moved from the kitchen in years and was covered in dust - even before the ceiling caved in. He bent down to turn on the radio, giving out a noise he'd never made before in his life - at least not as far as he was aware anyway. He brushed it off as old age getting to him and tuned the radio in - looking for any sign of life on the other side, even so much as an automated message would be comfort enough for him at this point. The radio flickered through channel after channel of either static or radio silence from rapidly abandoned stations that were left broadcasting - not that it made much of a difference anyway; people barely had enough time to make peace with whatever gods they believed in. Finally, Stephen found a station that was broadcasting. It was an automated message on repeat, probably sent from some government official cowering in some bunker miles underground - like a dragon from the days of yore, sitting atop their piles of gold and silver whilst the village people waste away in poverty outside. The message began to repeat, in a calm, cold, collected voice - "Stay inside your homes, and await further instruction".

Stephen scoffed at the message before turning the radio off. "As if people have anywhere to go anyway," he declared to no one in particular; "I don't imagine Brighton beach is a particularly popular holiday destination in the midst of all this".

His grumbling was quickly interrupted by Eva calling out from the kitchen, "Have you seen the nausea meds, darling? I feel awful".

Stephen paused and thought for a second. "Mark might know", he called back to her before rising to his feet with a drawn-out grunt of effort. Where was the boy anyway? It can't take long to arrange some pots and pans.

Outside, Mark stood and stared into the distance, surveying the rolling hills, the sparse trees and dead bushes that littered them, and the remains of animals in the fields that still lay where they fell. It all seemed so familiar, yet simultaneously it looked like a completely alien landscape. He found himself wondering if this had happened before, on some faraway planet. Was this what happened to make

Mars so dry and lifeless? As time goes on, history often repeats itself, so it isn't out of the question. "where am I again?" he asked the air in front of himself as if some booming voice of God would call out from the heavens to answer him.


Stephen ran his fingers through what hair he had in confusion upon seeing Mark stood there, talking to a fence. Stephen motioned to Eva to come outside with them, quickly realising that clumps of his hair had come out as he did. He threw them to the wayside, hoping they'd blow away in the wind before Eva noticed anything; His hair fell out as he got older - that was normal. But never in this volume. Eva found herself hiding secrets of her own inside the house; her hands fumbled and shook as she attempted to grip the doorknob. She took a deep breath and eventually forced her hand to comply, wiping any look of worry from her face before stepping outside. "That's new," she thought as she passed the threshold of the doorway, daintily stepping around various pots and pans. Her vision began to blur as the blood seemed to drain from her head rapidly. Her face turned ashen, and her lips paled as she collapsed - the ground rapidly rushing upward to catch her.

# Chapter Seven

Mark soon snapped out of his state of confusion and turned as he heard a feeble moan followed by the sound of Eva crumpling onto the patio. He had never moved so fast in his life as he rushed forth to check on Eva - "Mum!"
His words seemed to fall on deaf ears as she lay there; motionless, but groaning pathetically. Stephen grumbled something to himself inaudibly and began making his way through the long trek ahead of him - across the patio - with the vigour of a much younger man. Mark scrambled to check if Eva was okay, propping her head upon his lap as he pressed his fingers to her neck - desperately looking for a pulse. Stephen stopped dead in his tracks - something about the sight of his useless son fumbling about disagreed with him. He found himself doubled over, supporting his weight on knees that could barely handle that job at the best of times before vomiting. As much as he'd never let it show - the sanguine rivers that flowed from his mouth were what he feared the most; they told him there is no more hope. Stephen looked around at mark, despairingly searching for a distraction from the red mess spattered over his shoes - he found no respite; only mark staring back at him; who, for the first time, was seeing a glimpse of what seemed like vulnerability on his father's inscrutable countenance.

Mark lifted his mother's semi-conscious body gently, carrying her inside - while ineffectually trying to deny what he already knew. He lay her gently on the sofa. "Maybe some rest will do you good".

Mark turned from Eva as he spoke, hoping that would make his blatant lie less apparent. If nothing else, it would hide his reddening eyes.

Meanwhile, Stephen wiped the blood from around his mouth. He spat, hoping to rid himself of the metallic, acidic taste in his mouth - something he would typically condemn as a filthy habit for those damned unabashed youths and common criminals. Still, there aren't too many people present to judge through the end of the world. He stared down at the red puddle on his once flawless patio tiles and swallowed hard - he'd heard about these same things happening to people in Japan all those years ago. He sighed and shook his head disapprovingly at his situation as thunder rumbled in the distance - "There's no two ways 'bout it. I'll be dead in days", he announced to no one in particular - as if the vicious, pitiless, indifferent God that allowed this to happen to him and his family would descend from their pillar of gold people had placed them upon to cure that which ailed him. Stephen shook himself and steeled his jaw - he had to keep it together for Eva's sake. Stephen couldn't be seen as a hypocrite in front of the boy anyway - he peddled the age-old wisdom that real men don't cry, so he should live by it.

Stephen rushed towards the door - he was wasting what precious time Eva had left; he would never forgive himself if he wasted even more. However, he paused briefly at the door. For the smallest fraction of a second, he could have sworn he saw the faintest glimpse of something moving out of the very corner of his eye - something living, something angry. He brushed it off as nothing and raced inside - every second spent away from Eva was a second wasted - He ignored every creak from his worn, ancient bones and overlooked every complaint from each underused, weak muscle in his body bar none.

Some small part of Stephen's mind wished he hadn't. Eva was a sorry sight laying on the sofa. Pale and weak, barely clinging onto the last threads that kept her tied to the land of the living. Mark dragged his gaze up from his feet and turned to face Stephen, wiping the tears from his eyes - 'Real men don't cry, right?"
He spat the words at his father. Mark shook his head in disappointment and took a deep breath before locking eyes with Stephen for the first time in years. "She's dying. Fast".
Mark's words seemed to fall on deaf ears - serving only as a reminder of what Stephen already knew.

Stephen sighed as his gaze hit the floor; his stomach heaved, and his eyes burned. The air was quickly ripped from his lungs, and every muscle in his body turned taught at once, leaving him gasping for air like flailing about in vain on the land - drowning in the muggy air that surrounded him. He couldn't even find the will to face Mark. He had failed him, failed as a man.
His inner turmoil was quickly interrupted as something in Mark snapped - "Well?" He yelled with tears welling in his eyes before streaming down his cheeks in waves, "That's your wife! the mother of your children!". Spit flew from his mouth with each and every syllable as he continued, pacing about the room, "I always knew you felt nothing towards me, but I never knew you were so completely hollow".
'Say something!" Mark yelled, kicking the bucket in front of the shelter as Stephen shrank before his eyes. The bucket

rocked from the new sudden dent in its side, falling and spilling its contents across the floor, including the pistol that slid across the once pristine hardwood flooring, settling at Stephen's feet.

Mark's eyes naturally followed it across the floor, his gaze rising toward Stephen, though before anything resembling a word could leave his mouth, they were interrupted by someone - or something - crashing around in the kitchen. No sooner than Stephen had raised his head to reach for the gun at his feet and yell at Mark, something appeared in the doorway, its presence announced sharply by the sound of its thunderous steps in the hallway. It was big, it was angry, and it was out for blood. Stephen didn't care - nothing would stand between him and the creature until one or both of them was dead. He had failed to protect his family once already, and that wasn't about to happen again.

# Chapter 8

The creature stood in the doorway, muscle fibres twitching and flexing just beneath its skin. It was covered in dirty, matted hair missing in large swathes all across its body which fell out before their eyes, leaving ugly bald patches of pale skin that showed through a spiderweb of interconnecting scars and blood vessels. It carried a stench of burning hair as it took a few confident steps through the door, exposing patches of charred, black leathery skin - which in places was beginning to slough off - as well as open bleeding gashes across its body. Gnarled, twisted horns rose from its head, stained in overlapping shades of black, yellow and red.

Stephen stood his ground, forcing his muscles, weakened by age, to comply and raise the gun at the creature, as he yelled at Mark - "get in the shelter, boy. I'll deal with this". Mark didn't have to be told twice, practically diving through the open end of the shelter, quickly crawling inside, pressing his back to the wall, as if that would do much to stop the monster that stood before them. Stephen locked eyes with the creature, gritting his teeth and squeezing the trigger slightly - it seemed to recognise the challenge by Stephen, stopping in its tracks and meeting his gaze. It had finally found a worthy challenger.

Moments seemed to crawl like hours as they stood there, locked in an unspoken battle of sheer grit and determination, albeit one that could only ever end one way. There'd be no negotiating a peaceful end to this battle; their life and death game of chicken would ultimately be a bloody one.

The beast lowered its head, stepping back, readying itself to attack. Time seemed to slow - chemicals flooded Stephen's brain, preparing his body to either fight for his life or die with honour. The creature rocked backwards onto its hind legs, like a spring winding up, ready to launch itself into and subsequently through Stephen in an instant - almost like clockwork, his finger pulled back against the trigger, again and again. He unloaded into the top of the beast's skull, shredding through its tough skin and thick bone, destroying the soft, squishy precious cargo that its skull encapsulated, ultimately killing it - leaving only one round left chambered in the gun. A tragic end to a once majestic creature, though, humanity always did have a certain dexterity, a mastery of destroying nature - no matter how unnatural that nature may be. The blasts resounded out across the land - past dead trees from which no birds fled in terror, along the malformed roads, bouncing around the empty town, where nothing seemed to be still living, though someone - something - stirred in the darkness of half-destroyed buildings. Things that were no longer altogether human. They echoed out across empty meadows and leas filled with nothing more than bones and burnt grass over the steppes and rolling barren plains. Reaching as far as the neighbouring towns.

Three men decked out from head to toe in camouflage, and protective gear hiked along the main road leading from South Thill - another small town near the coast, albeit a more popular destination than Oymor Bay for some inexplicable reason. One man, with the name on his shirt reading 'Horton', pulled a radio from his belt and raised it near his face, finally breaking the silence - "Echo one, this is Raven, South Thill is empty, no survivors at all".

His voice was rough but still betrayed a sense of hopelessness, a sense of disillusionment with their charge - it wasn't exactly likely there were many survivors, if any. Another of the men, his shirt emblazed with the name Daniels', fought with a map of the area, pulling a marker pen from his pocket and ran a line through South Thill - many of the surrounding towns were also marked in the same way; Stonesteig, St. Calne, West Keswath; once lively towns and cities, now ghost towns, devoid of *most* signs of life. Much like Ozymandias' statue, nothing beside stood but the burnt-out husks of the old stone cottages that once dotted the hillsides. Horton's radio crackled to life, breaking the crushing silence once again - "Raven, this is Echo One. Aren't you meant to say nevermore? Prior transmission is noted. You are advised to avoid Reppals, it's to be considered no man's land".

Horton whispered "prick" under his breath and turned to see Daniels already marking it on the map. They returned promptly to their walking, heading toward Bridbextow when the cracking sound of gunfire rang out across the hills. Instinctively they crouched, turned to face the noise and drew their weapons - Daniels picked the map up from the floor and withdrew a compass. "Oymor Bay".

He looked over at Horton through the small glass eye-holes in the front of his mask, "Well, just outside it anyway", he smirked under his mask, "so we heading out then, Lenore?".

Horton took a second to mull it over before nodding to the other two men, withdrawing the radio once more - "Echo One, This is Raven. We've heard gunshots from the outskirts of Oymor Bay, could suggest survivors. Please advise".
The men started walking toward the sound as the radio crackled to life once again - "Raven, this is Echo One. Be advised, Oymor Bay is danger close. The last team sent there have gone radio silent. Proceed with caution".
The third man of the group, Welch, finally broke his bout of stoic silence - "Well shit, looks like we're gonna have some fun with this".

Stephen walked over and kicked the lifeless head of the beast that now lay on the floor before them - it rocked lifelessly to the side. "Well. All the work John put into raising that prize bull paid off, I guess".

Mark crawled from the shelter, standing slowly, never taking his eyes off the hulking behemoth that lay before them, mere feet from his mother's now lifeless body. Stephen practically collapsed into an armchair across the room as Mark stood there, unable to take his eyes off the beast lying in the doorway, unable to comprehend how nature could create something like that. His line of thought was soon interrupted as Stephen began hacking in the corner behind him. However, Mark was fixated on watching the beast, as if there were some chance that it may get up again; meanwhile, Stephen bit his tongue and wiped his hand on his trousers - leaving a deep red stain down the side of his leg. Neither one of them spoke for what felt like hours but amounted to nothing more than mere minutes before Mark finally split the thunderous silence, gesturing vaguely in the direction of the creature - "What in the actual fuck did they put in those bombs to create... That".

## Chapter 9

Stephen dutifully almost mechanically moved toward Eva, picking up a mostly clean sheet from the floor, draping it over her body. He paused as he reached her neck - whispering a prayer as his trembling hand moved to close her eyes - "I'll see you soon, darling. Don't you worry, I won't be keeping Charon waiting long". He swallowed his tears before they could leave his eyes and covered her face; "There'll be another star in the sky tonight, Mark. Make sure to wave" - he sighed as he spoke, the words falling uselessly from his mouth.

Steven steeled himself and moved away, stepping over the creature in the doorframe and moving out into the kitchen, followed silently by Mark as they trudged across the garden toward the shed, both knowing what they had to do, but neither one willing to admit it.

The wooden shafts of the shovels felt cold in their hands, and the silence between them was broken only by the delicate crunching sound of the blades piercing the soil beneath their feet; or the intermittent grunting sounds coming from Steven as he occasionally re-adjusted his grip, struggling to hold onto the shovel. Mark finally spoke out, for the first time in what felt like hours - "She would hate us digging up her flower bed".

Steven responded with a grunt, afraid of what may follow any words leaving his mouth, and so Mark continued - "It's the best place though. She always did love her gardening".

Minutes seemed to pass as days in the once again crushing silence until they were satisfied the hole was deep enough nothing could get to Eva - If that thing in the hallway could exist, then God only knows what else could be out there and hungry.

Horton led the rest of the Raven Team across the marshes - passing between two buildings and heading into Oymor Bay, stopping abruptly and reaching for his radio - "Echo One, this is Raven. We're passing through Oymor Bay now. Danger close, Echo One should expect radio silence". Moving as a tight group, they walked past dark, burnt-out husks of storefronts and wreaked, rusted cars laying motionless on top of cracked roads. Welch found himself staring at the rubble that now sat piled up where there was once a church, charred parts of pews stuck out from the ruins, as well as things he wished he hadn't seen. Horton slapped him on the back, bringing him sharply back to reality with a jump. "Come on. We're burning daylight here. You know what's gonna be crawling around in those shops; I'd rather not be here when the sun goes down and they come out to play."

Welch nodded and shook himself. He'd much rather not have another run-in with the blinders if he didn't have to.

Steven clutched his chest and moved to the sofa, laying down as he struggled to pull breath into his lungs through the choking dust that hung in the air and surrounded them. Meanwhile, Mark paced back and forth, talking and gesturing to no one in particular as if he were communing with unseen forces. Stephen weakly called out to Mark, using what little of the heavy air he could hold - Mark rushed over, seeing the sorry state his father was in - "What's happening" he gasped.

Stephen looked over at him and shakily pushed the gun into Mark's hands - "I kept this gun from my army days. That's where I met your mother, you know?" He took a second to catch his breath; speaking in full sentences seemed to drain him. "I ended up in the infirmary tent. Thought it was the worst thing that could've happened. But then there she was". Tears welled in Stephen's eyes as he lay there, struggling to continue - "Your mother could always tell when it was someone's time. I'm in pain mark. It's my time. I need you to help me get there."

Tears welled in Mark's eyes as the realisation of what was being asked of him swept over him, but still, Stephen continued - "I wish I didn't have to leave you like this, but I made a promise. I told Eva I wouldn't keep her waiting." Mark motioned for him to stop talking. Stephen's voice was thin and raspy; every breath he took seemed to send waves of pain rocking across his body. Mark knew what he had to do.

The metal grip felt as if it were razing his hands as he held it; the gun was heavier than he thought it would have been and only seemed to get bulkier as he raised it, placing the cold metal barrel against Stephen's forehead, moving his finger to the trigger. Stephen looked up into his eyes as a tear rolled down Mark's cheek. With the last breath he would ever take, he decided to set things straight with his son. "I was always proud of you", He panted. Then with a loud crack, everything went dark.

Outside, Raven Team started sprinting up the hill, past rows of dead hedges and razed, blank fields of dead grass - weapons bared as Horton called out - "weapons hot, I see movement".

Mark dropped the gun and backed away slowly, wrestling with a thousand thoughts running through his mind - deciding on one. "I have to get away".

He ran towards that burnt front door, pausing only briefly to look back at the house he grew up in one last time, committing it to memory, as surely this would be the last time he saw it. He stepped through the front door and collapsed into a mess on the front doorstep, wracked with guilt and complicated emotions as three men ran up the road.

Raven Team kept their weapons solidly trained on Mark as he sat there weeping before lowering them, deciding he'd pose no threat. Mark looked up at them, with tears in his eyes and croaked out - "They're all dead. There's nothing left. Take what you want, just leave me be".

Horton reached for his radio - "Echo One. This is Raven. One survivor in Oymor Bay, Returning to base." Welch extended a hand in Mark's direction and spoke as gently as he could through a gruff South-Eastern accent - "Come with us, lad. We can take you somewhere safe".

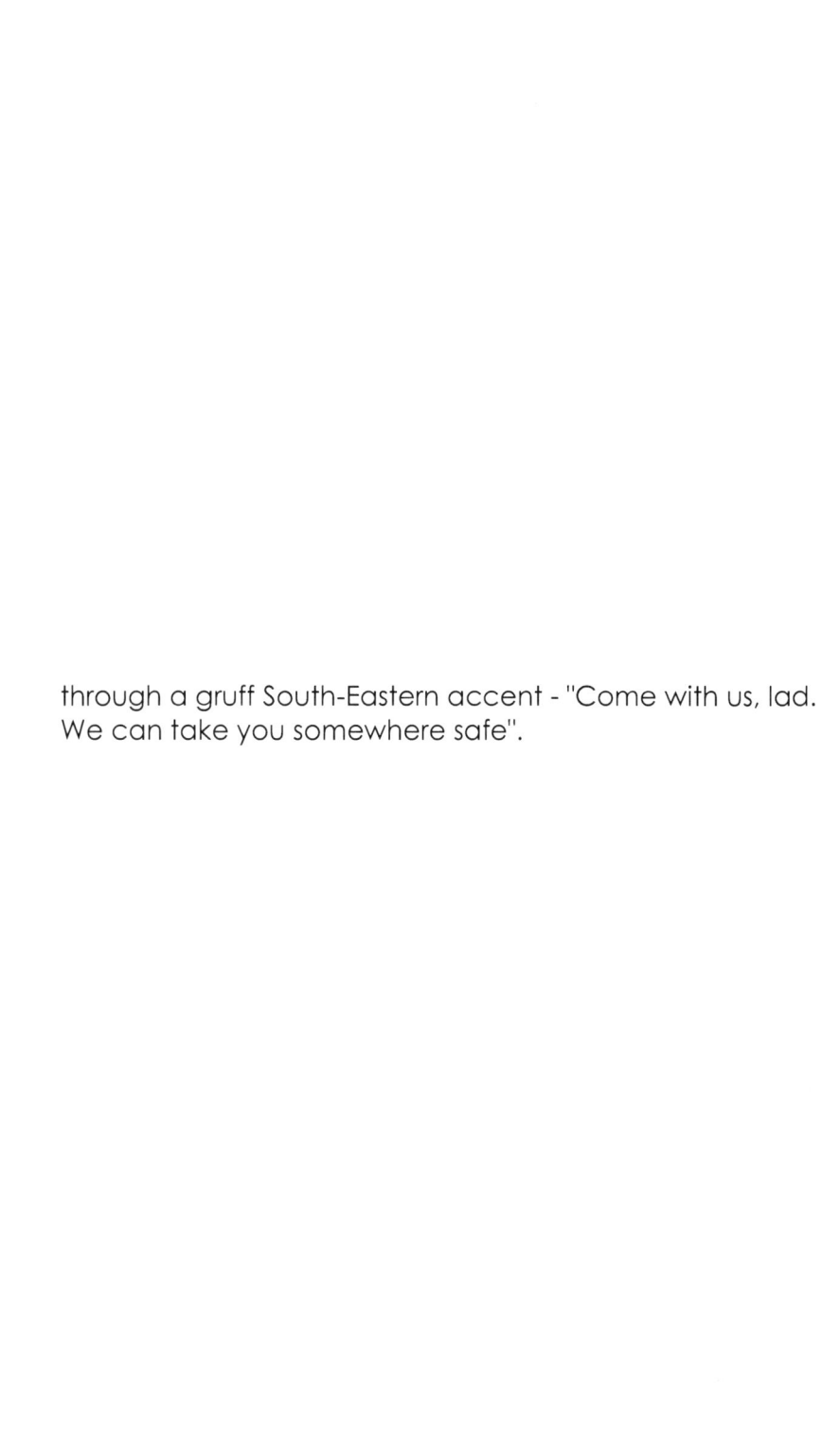

Printed in Great Britain
by Amazon